Jonas Cook

Uncle Jonas Talks

Jonas Cook

Uncle Jonas Talks

ISBN/EAN: 9783743377943

Manufactured in Europe, USA, Canada, Australia, Japa

Cover: Foto ©Andreas Hilbeck / pixelio.de

Manufactured and distributed by brebook publishing software
(www.brebook.com)

Jonas Cook

Uncle Jonas Talks

UNCLE JONAS.

BY

JONAS COOK,

EDITOR HARPER SENTINEL.

———————

HARPER, KANSAS.

HARPER SENTINEL, PUBLISHER.

1891.

TO THE PUBLIC.

The articles contained in this little volume appeared in the HARPER SENTINEL during the fall and winter of 1890 and '91. They were received with such favor that their author concluded to put them in book form.

In the hope that those who read this little book may find some thoughts worthy of attention the author gives it to the public.

JONAS COOK.

Harper, Kansas, May 10, 1891.

CONTENTS.

OPPOSITION.

Opposition, my dear friends, is not the worst thing that can come to a man. In fact, it is more frequently a benefit than an injury. It is too often the case that the very things we want and the very principles we advocate would be the worst for us if we should get them.

The little child that tries to grasp the burning lamp would be badly injured, were it not for the mother's opposition. The boy's kite would fall to the ground were it not for the opposition of the wind.

Had the English government not opposed the colonists, America might be to-day feeding the British lion and trembling at his roar. Had not Jefferson Davis opposed the terms of Lincoln's emancipation proclamation, the auction block with all its horrors and the cruel lash upon the back of the slave, might be things of the present instead of the past.

Opposition shows a man his weak points, and if he is made of good material, he will seek to strengthen his weakness and rise above obstacles thrown in his way.

Opposition awakens thought, stimulates ambition and leads onward and upward.

Do not, my dear friends, confound persecution and oppression with opposition. They are very different things. Opposition may be void of both malice and injustice.

The fond mother who holds the nose of her child while she forces it to take medicine in opposition to its wishes, is not prompted by any malicious or unjust feeling toward it, but she knows she must oppose the child's wishes in order to accomplish its greatest good.

Just so in life, if we will but look beyond our feelings into our reason and judgment, we will find that opposition is more frequently a benefit than an injury.

GONE TO SEED.

My Dear Friends: You, no doubt, have heard and used the expression "gone to seed" in reference to the vegetables in your garden. Did you ever think what it means? When a plant has gone to seed, it simply means it has ceased to grow, and all that is left of it are the germs or seeds of reproduction. In fact, the plant has finished its mission here, and will soon return to nourish mother earth whence it came.

Have you ever observed that there are a great many people in this world who are like the plants—they have gone to seed?

In fact, the world is full of men and women who have ceased to grow, socially, morally, or intellectually, and it may be justly said of them, they have gone to seed.

In your mind's eye, my dear friends; look across the barbed-wire fence into the field known as school teaching, and see how many of your acquaintances in that vocation have gone to seed. Do you not find men and women there who do not seem to have improved one iota by long years in the school room? Do you not even find that they know no more now than they did when you first formed their acquaintance?

Well, these folks are done growing. The vital sap has ceased to circulate, and they have gone to seed, and ought to be removed from the school room.

Now, cast your eye around you and see how many lawyers there are who belong to that class who have gone to seed. Do you not see them on all sides? Do you not observe that a majority of them have settled down to a kind of routine business which requires no effort that will cause them to reach out in their profession? Well, these fellows have gone to seed, and are of but little use to society—except as consumers of agricultural products, and swellers of the census. If dying naturally was an act of the will, they could benefit society by performing that act.

Now, my dear friends, meander with your Uncle Jonas in the theological garden for a few minutes, and let us look around and see how many plants are there that have gone to seed. Don't you see a great many who have ceased to receive nourishment from the fertile soil of the Sermon on the Mount, and have gone to seed on creed? Yea, verily, it has ever been thus.

But, my dear friends, let us leave this garden and go into the political field. There is no place where so many human plants who have gone to seed can be found as in politics. In fact, they have shot to seed so quickly that the seed is not even sound, and but few of them in the pod; and the pod often gaps open, and as the wind whistles through it, nothing is heard save the sound of emptiness. The average human plant grows but little politically. It may be on account of the soil in which it is planted—but be that as it may, you will observe that this field is full of human plants that have gone to seed.

Yes, my dear friends, you will find in all the gardens of life a great many plants that have gone to seed, and many of them have become so old that they rattle in the pod.

There is no need of so many people ceasing to grow intellectually as there are. There is enough food for thought to keep them growing, were it not for pure, unadulterated mental laziness.

Your Uncle Jonas advises you not to go to seed too early in life.

WHO ARE PATRIOTS ?

My Dear Friends: There seems to be an opinion in this fair land of ours that war and gunpowder, shot and shell, sword and bayonet, grapeshot and canister, blood and carnage must, in some way, be connected with a man's history before he is entitled to the crown of a patriot.

There seems to be an idea that in times of peace, patriots do not exist, and that a man must smell gunpowder on the field of battle, or cool coffee around a camp-fire if he would deserve to be called a patriot.

Your Uncle is aware that the man who goes forth to defend his country when it is threatened by an enemy deserves praise and honor, and he generally gets it if he has to give it to himself.

But, you, no doubt, have observed that there are a great many men who want to own the country they have defended in time of war, and by their actions and conduct after peace has been declared, are doing but little to preserve in peace what they won in battle.

Yes, my dear friends, it was patriotic for

men to face the cannon's mouth in order that "our country should be kept upon the map of the world and our flag floating in the breezes of heaven." It was a duty they owed to their homes and the generations to follow,—but it is not patriotism for any class of men to ask too much for doing their duty.

No nation under the broad canopy of heaven has been as grateful to her soldiers as this nation has been and is at the present day.

Your Uncle desires to see every man who was disabled while defending his country, cared for properly,—but he has little respect for that man who spends his pension money for beer and liquor and transforms his home into a hell. He is not a patriot now who acts thus—even though he left a part of his anatomy upon the battle field.

There is such a thing as asking too much. There is such a thing as patriots being transformed into mendicants and demanding pay for services which they never rendered. Like a man in Pennsylvania who applied for a pension because his substitute was wounded.

Are not the man and woman who make their home happy—who rear a good, honest, truthful, intelligent family—who lead a straightforward life, wronging no one—

building a national defence which grows stronger as time passes by, just as good and noble patriots as they who shoulder a musket and go forth to battle?

Your Uncle Jonas has but little use for a patriotism that only swells on the 4th of July and Decoration Day. He likes a patriotism that will build happy and prosperous homes, —a patriotism that will cause men to educate their children—a patriotism that will purify the ballot box—a patriotism that will purify the voter.

When this nation has that kind of patriots in time of peace, she will never have cause for cruel war. My dear friends, are you patriots?

HOW.

My Dear Friends: Your Uncle has observed that people receive more in this world for knowing HOW to do work than for doing it.

A large manufacturing establishment was once closed down because the engine and machinery, from some unknown cause, would not do their work. The men in charge sought in vain to learn the trouble, and repair where necessary—but they could not find the cause of the engine's refusing to do its work. Workmen by the scores were standing idle and the owners of the establishment had large contracts that were to be filled—a failure of which meant financial disaster.

There was a skillful and ingenious man living in the city. He was sent for and came. He examined the machinery, loosened a nut here, and tightened one there, scrutinizing everything with eye and ear, and in a short time the machinery was in motion and the men all at work.

He was called to the office and asked what he charged for repairing the machinery.. He replied, ."I worked two and one half hours,

for which I charge $2.50,—but for knowing
HOW to do it, I charge you $97.50.   Total,
$100.00.''

The bill was paid without a murmur and
money saved the owners by so doing.

My dear friends, your Uncle Jonas has
observed that the person who knows how to
do work, can do it much more easily, and
with less waste of muscular power than he
who attempts to do it by "main strength and
awkwardness."

The physician who examines your pulse
and writes you a prescription does not charge
you much for his work, but he charges for
knowing how.   If a leg or arm is to be am-
putated, a common butcher with his saw
could do the job so far as the mere work is
concerned as easily as he can saw a beef bone
—but the surgeon is called because he knows
how to do it without endangering the life of
the person.

My dear friends, this age demands more of
a person than mere muscular power.   He
must be skilled in some way.   He must
know how to use his strength to a purpose.
His education must be not only of the hand,
but of the head also.

The winds of heaven sported overhead for

thousands of years before man learned how to yoke them to the piston of his pump and make them do his bidding.

It took thousands of years for man to discover how to imprison steam and make it "turn with tireless arm the countless wheels of toil."

Many centuries came and went, before man learned how to capture electricity and make it the fleetest messenger the world has ever known.

Your Uncle has oftimes thought that the forces which seem so potent of evil would be just as potent of good if we only knew how to apply them. The same knife that cuts your bread and meat might cut your throat. It all depends upon how it is applied.

My dear friends, when you are passing along your journey of life, you will find that it is of just as much importance for you to know how to do and how to act, as it is for you to know what to do and when and where to do it.

The average man's "hindsight is much better than his foresight" and it does not take much ability to explain how a thing was done after it is done.

The world is full of men who are standing

with their hands thrust into the pockets of their jeans up to the elbows, and informing the dear people what ought to be done, but have not even the ghost of an idea how it can be accomplished.

The eminent lawyer receives a large fee for knowing how to handle his case; the eminent teacher for knowing how to teach and manage; the eminent preacher for knowing how to preach, and so on from Alpha to Omaha.

So, my dear friends, if you desire to become something more than a mere "thing of beauty and a jaw forever," you must commingle your thoughts with your work—you must plan and execute—you must study HOW to do and then do it.

RASHNESS OF THE MOUTH.

My Dear Friends: No doubt, you have observed that there is a disease which is very contagious, and which exists in every clime that the wand of civilization has touched, and for want of a medical term your Uncle will call it "Rashness of the Mouth."

There are a great number of people afflicted WITH it, and a much larger number afflicted BY it.

In some cases it is hereditary and in other cases it is acquired.

It quite often kills the victim who is afflicted with it and cripples those who are afflicted by it. This rashness of the mouth is sometimes cured by the fellow's fist who is affected by it, coming in contact with the person's mouth who has it, with such force as to horizontalize his perpendicularity.

Like the consumption, it steals unawares upon people and gnaws at their social life to such an extent that their eyes become gangrened with hatred—they lose confidence in their fellow beings, and there is a breaking out at the mouth, and the air is filled with social and moral miasma.

When a person has a bad case of rashness of the mouth it is generally accompanied by a very fertile imagination, which leads him to talk about everybody's business but his own, and does it, too, in an uncomplimentary manner.

This afflicted class generally obey the following injunctions:

> " Tell your neighbors all you know,
> Who it was that told you so;
> Talk to this one, talk to that,
> Learn your story, get it pat."

This disease is very contagious among people who have more mouth than brains.

This rashness of the mouth is quite often preceded by two other diseases; namely: petrifaction of the heart and putrefaction of the brain.

My dear friends, to be honest in this matter, we are all more or less afflicted with the rashness of the mouth. We too often are ready and willing without thinking what the result will be, to assist in circulating an evil report on our fellow beings before we know whether it is true or not.

The little verse which follows your Uncle committed some years ago:

"First somebody told it,
  Then the room wouldn't hold it;
And the busy tongues rolled it,
  Till they got it outside.
When the crowd came across it,
  They never once lost it,
But tossed it and tossed it,
  Till it grew lŏng and wide."

How often do people become rash at the
mouth because somebody told this or that
and before the truth could be learned, it
grows "long and wide."

When an evil report is heard, my dear
friends, would it not be best for us to ask, "Is
it true?" and if true, "Is it a benefit to society to tell it?"   If these two questions were
asked candidly, your Uncle believes that
there would be fewer cases of the rashness of
the mouth than there are.

"Speak gently to the erring—know,
  They may have toiled in vain;
Perchance unkindness made them so.
  Oh, win them back again."

My dear friends, this rashness of the mouth
has destroyed the happiness of many a home.
It has changed love into hatred.   It has arrayed husband against wife—children against
parents—friend against friend.   It has often
taken out of life all that is worth living for,
and obscured the Star of Hope in life's firma-

ment and left nothing but the darkness of despair.

When your Uncle sees some poor wayfaring person who has strayed from the path of duty and who has lost his self-respect, he often thinks it may be more the fault of society —more the fault of the rashness of other's mouths than that of his own. Many persons are too weak to bear the severe censure of their fellow beings without straying from the path of duty.

My dear friends, your Uncle Jonas advises you to be careful how you handle words. They are dangerous things. "The tongue has cut off more heads than the sword." When you feel that you are about to be seized with rashness of the mouth, as an antidote ponder well the following verse of Will Carlton:

"Boys flying kites may haul in their white-
   winged birds,
You can't do that way when you are flying words.
'Careful with fire' is good advice, I know,
'Careful with words' is ten times doubly so.
Thoughts unexpressed may fall back dead,
God, himself, cannot kill them when they're said.

Yes, the small pox is preferable to a severe case of the rashness of the mouth.

WILL IT PAY?

My Dear Friends: When the Creator stood with the clay in his hands and the idea in his mind ready to make man in his own image, it is likely that he asked himself the question, Will it pay?

Will it pay to create a being capable of loving and hating, hoping and fearing—capable of doing right and wrong—capable of bearing pleasure and pain—capable of ascending the scale of progression or descending to the depths of degradation?

Man who was made in the image of his Maker generally asks himself, when about to do anything, "Will it pay?" "Wherein will I be benefited if I pursue this or that course?" "Will it pay for me to undertake this enterprise or will I reap a greater reward by doing something else?"

These questions, your Uncle has observed, have been asked by men viewing the rewards from different standpoints. The majority of men when they propound the question, Will it pay? to themselves have in mind a material reward—one of dollars and cents. They seem to look upon the accumulation of prop-

erty to satisfy some personal or selfish ambition as the only real answer to the question,
Will it pay?   They have a greater desire to
rise above their fellow man than to raise him
to a higher plane in the social world.

My dear friends, the greatest reward for
work does not always come in dollars and
cents, but in the full consciousness of having
assisted others or having aided your fellow
man to a nobler life.

You cannot afford to neglect the little acts
of kindness toward your associates—you cannot afford to neglect to speak a kind word to
those you daily meet—many of whom are
soul-sick and almost too weak to bear the
burdens of life.   Will it pay to withhold from
such the balm of sympathy which will
encourage them to better deeds?

Too many people believe in immediate
returns for their work—the Jonah's gourd
kind that comes in a night, and they do not
seem to think that it will pay to cast their
bread upon the waters with the expectation
that it will return after many days.

A number of years ago (pardon reference
to self) your Uncle was the teacher of a
young man who had but little home attrac-
tions.   He longed to tear himself away from

his country home, so he came to town and in a short time was frequenting the saloons—a thing that was not considered in that place as being much disgrace if any. Being confident of the fact that the boy had a great deal of respect for his teacher's opinion, your Uncle met him alone one day when about the following advice was given him in the most friendly manner: "I saw you going in and coming out of saloons several times. You cannot ever expect to become much of a man if you frequent such places. I presume you have been drinking some. I do not fault you for going in to see what is there—but you ought not to go as a customer. Look around you and see the men in this town who a few years ago were honored and respected and whom you now know as drunkards. Now, when you get out by yourself, I want you to ask yourself this question, 'Can I afford to take any risks in becoming like them?' "

Years after the above advice was given and the boy had gone out into the busy world, and your Uncle had lost trace of him, a letter came stating that he had a good position paying him one hundred dollars per month, and amongst other things he wrote, "I have

never tasted an intoxicating drink since the
day you gave me that little advice, and I
suppose if it had not been for you I would
be a drunkard.''

My dear friends, there was no money in
the above work for your Uncle,—but he has
been paid a thousand fold for what he did for
that boy.

Will it pay to let .boys and girls, young
men and young women go to ruin when but
a few words given in the proper spirit, by
the right person at the right time, in the
right manner and at the right place, will
save them?

Will it pay to follow a business that simply
clothes the back and feeds the stomach?   Do
not think for a moment your Uncle Jonas
would take from man the desire to accumulate property and make money—for by obser-
vation he has learned that those who work to
accumulate wealth are amongst the best people on earth.   But men can work and accumulate and not neglect to assist those around
them who need advice—who need a word of
encouragement—who need sympathy.

Too many men have fallen into the habit
of passing by boys without noticing them—
snubbing them on every occasion.   It does

not pay to act thus. These boys soon become men, and an injustice or an uncalled for snub done a boy, he never forgets it when he becomes a man. Your Uncle is now speaking from experience.

My dear friends, will it pay to treat your fellow man in an uncivil manner? Will it pay to be selfish and arrogant? Will it pay never to lend a helping hand to those in need? Will it pay to use any power you may possess for any other purpose than to promote the best possible good? Will it pay to accumulate wealth at the expense of honesty and the true principles of manhood? Will it pay to conduct yourself in such a manner that when old age—the time for reflection—comes upon you that you will be forced to review a life full of selfish deeds?

KEEP OFF THE GRASS.

My Dear Friends: Did you ever pass through a public park without seeing on every turn the command to "keep off the grass?" This sign is stuck up everywhere in cities until people are almost led to believe that grass is not to be trod upon at all.

At the opening of the Chicago schools a few weeks ago, a little six-year-old boy who had spent the most of the summer in the parks and had been compelled to stare at the keep-off-the-grass placards, started to school and the teacher was talking to her pupils concerning the earth and the many beautiful things that grow thereon, and while she was speaking of the beautiful grass that covers the earth like a carpet, one little hand came up and he said: "Teacher, I know what grass is."

The teacher smiling, asked "What is it, Charlie?"

Charlie replied, "Grass is something that people must keep off of."

Your Uncle never sees one of these keep-off-the-grass cards that he does not feel like tramping it. While he is aware that it is necessary sometimes to say "Thus far—but no farther," yet people are ordered to keep off the grass by so many commanders that have commissioned themselves to give orders and their right is only assumed.

My dear friends, while your Uncle has been roaming around in the green pastures of society, lo, these many years, he has been confronted with this same keep-off-the-grass spirit that is to be seen on placards in the park.

If a man or class of men resolve to cut loose from an old political party, even though its principles have lost their usefulness by time, there will be a howl go up in loud tones that they keep off the grass and return to the beaten paths of their old party. The self-constituted policemen of the old party will swing their political maces of sneers and abuse above their heads and command all to keep off the grass in the political park.

Occasionally a barbed wire is stretched between the grass and the beaten path, so he who attempts to cross over into the green pastures may rend his garments.

This keep-off-the-grass card is also seen in the religious parks of the world, and the man or class of men in all ages, who have strayed from the paths of the majority have been called upon to keep in line and not trample on the grass on either side.

Yes, my friends, the parks of society in this world are filled with orders to keep off the grass.

When Dr. Harvey announced to the world that the blood of man circulated in his body the entire medical fraternity yelled at him to keep off the grass. To-day there is not a physician in the land but what knows that Dr. Harvey was correct in his statement.

When our Revolutionary fathers sought to establish a "government for the people, of the people, and by the people," a pusillanimous, bull-headed king ordered them to keep off the grass, and he attempted to enforce his order by the "last argument to which kings resort."

Your Uncle has observed that there are too many cards posted up in this world telling people what NOT to do instead of telling them what to do. In society matters people bow to customs quite often that are as absurd as anything can be, simply for fear that they may trample on the grass outside of the worn path.

Public opinion is a mediocre—a tyrant

quite often that would crush out all progress if possible. Public opinion has transformed many a budding genius into a blatant hypocrite. Your Uncle is aware, however, that a good healthy public opinion is the conservative power—the balance-wheel of society—yet there is a great deal of public opinion that is not of a good healthy kind, judging from the effect it produces.

This keep-off-the-grass card is found in too many homes. Your Uncle has visited houses that were called homes where the children were not allowed to enjoy themselves for fear of soiling the carpet, scarring the furniture, or tearing the lace curtains. They could not turn around without being told "to be careful," "don't do that," "that's naughty," "don't soil the carpet," etc., etc., until the sweet milk of concord in the household had become sour, and home (?) had no charms for them.

My dear friends, men have always differed in opinion on great and small subjects, and your Uncle is glad such is true, but that is no reason men should not be tolerant with each other—that is no reason men should hate each other—that is no reason they should order each other to keep off the grass.

The continent of Thought is infinitely large, and there is room for all without each person putting up the sign keep off the grass and as time goes by and men become truly civilized, as your Uncle believes they will, then, and not till then, will people no more be ordered to keep off the grass.

BUZZARD AND HUMMING-BIRD.

My Dear Friends: Many years ago when your Uncle was a small boy living among the vine-clad hills of his eastern Ohio home, he was cutting down mullen stalks which had grown upon the field; and beautiful flowers were in bloom and all nature was giving evidence that autumn was at hand. The orchard near by was groaning under its load of Wall-dower, Rambo and other apples of the choicest kind. The robin and swallow were preparing to migrate to a warmer clime. The busy bee was chasing from flower to flower, gathering his winter store of honey. The crow was cawing in the woods beyond. The frisky little squirrel was chattering as he stored away the nuts. The grasshopper was ceasing to be a burden and the little ant was hurrying to and fro busy with its work which no human can understand, and as your Uncle lay there under the old wild cherry tree, his scythe by his side watching these members of the lower creation and dreaming only such day visions as boys can dream, a great large buzzard came flying over his head. He watched it as it balanced itself upon the atmospheric sea and sailed as gracefully as a ship over the placid waters of a lake. It seemed to take no notice of the flowers that were blooming in the fields or the beauties of nature that were around on every side. But in a short time it saw the object of its search and hovering above it for a moment then lighted upon it.

It was the carcass of an old dead sheep which lay in one corner of the field. Your Uncle watched it as it feasted with a great deal of delight upon the putrid flesh, the stench of which but a short time before had driven the boy who was lying beneath the wild cherry tree from that portion of the field. While musing over the strange nature of the buzzard and chiding it for lacking in taste, a beautiful little humming-bird came flitting by, diving its tiny bill into a flower here and hovering over a flower there, and sipping the nectar and in a gleesome manner seeming to enjoy the beauties which surrounded it on every side.

The buzzard having satisfied its appetite sailed away and was seen no more. The humming-bird was soon lost to sight, and the boy picked up his scythe and resumed his work of cutting the mullen, little thinking, then that he had gathered food for thought from the buzzard and the humming-bird which in after years could be applied as a lesson in life.

My dear friends, long years have come and gone since that day, and as your Uncle has traveled over many states which then had no location to him except on the map in his text-book in geography, he has seen and met some human buzzards who fly over the field of society, which is filled with many beautiful things, scenting the air not for the pure, but for the putrid and decaying matter they may find. These human buzzards, though few in number, may be seen moving about every day with no eye to see that which is good— no scent to smell that which is wholesome— no desire to partake of that which is pure. On the other hand, your Uncle has seen and met ninety-nine human humming-birds to one buzzard, who like the humming-bird of his boyhood days fly over the field and see the beauties—taste of the sweets, and never once think of feasting upon the dead and putrefying bodies that lie in the fence corners of this field of human society.

My dear friends, you can each transform

yourself into a human buzzard if you desire—
you can educate yourself to see nothing that
is pure, noble, and good in your fellow man
—you can make yourself miserable by refusing
to taste of the sweets of life, or you each can
be a humming-bird if you so desire—you can
educate yourself to see that there is a great
deal more good than evil—more of the pure
than of the impure—more happiness than
unhappiness in this field of human society.

The buzzard of the bird kingdom no doubt
has a mission to perform which is of as much
importance as that of the humming-bird's, but
this buzzard never feasts on anything until it
is really dead, while the human buzzard
preys quite often upon the supposed dead and
putrid matter of society.

Your Uncle leaves this subject with you
allowing you each to choose for yourself
whether you will be a buzzard or humming-
bird in society.

GOOD PEOPLE.

My Dear Friends: When you go home after your day's work is done you are apt to sit down and think of the mean things that your fellow-men have done that day. You are apt to think harshly of the acts or imagined acts of those you have met. Man is prone to consider that his fellow-man is seeking to take some advantage of him when, in fact, these thoughts are too often but a reflection of self.

When you go home some evening sit down in solitude, with a lead pencil in hand, and write out the names of those you met that day, and when you have done that, then draw a line across the names of those who have done you an injury or mistreated you in any way, and your Uncle will venture the assertion that you will be surprised how few the number.

Why, my dear friends, this world is so full of good and noble people that it is sometimes a pleasure, by way of change, to meet a person who has a surplus of pure, unadulterated meanness about him and in him. It has a tendency to make one appreciate good people.

Your Uncle has been a resident of this city more than three years, and he meets hundreds of different persons every day, and some days thousands, and in all that time he has met but one man in this city whom he positively knows has done him an injury. But when he thinks over how much a mean man must suffer for his meanness—how dreadful it must be for a person to be in company with mean thoughts concerning himself —he would rather be the one who is mistreated than he who mistreats. In such a case it is more blessed to receive than to give.

But, oh, how many good people has your Uncle met in the same time. As he passes up and down the streets daily he often thinks the world is full of good people, and he has no desire to leave it. He feels like the Kansas farmer when attending a revival meeting, and the minister called on all those who wanted to go to heaven to rise. All rose but the farmer, and when the minister walked down the aisle with the lachrymose substance trickling down his cheeks, and taking the farmer by the hand said: "My dear brother, when I asked all to rise who wanted to go to heaven, you did not get up. Why this thusness?''

The farmer replied in tones that could be heard all over the house, "Wal, I'll tell you. I want to stay right here in Kansas. This is good enough for me."

This is a kind old world and kind people living in it, if you only do your part.

Of course, mistakes are often made and wrongs done, but it may be that these are what make us love the right and the true. The most of the evil in this world is too often imaginary.

Mr. Shakespeare says, "There is nothing either right or wrong but thinking makes it so."

Your Uncle does not wholly agree with Shakespeare, yet he thinks that nine times out of ten his saying just quoted is true.

Persons too often consider other people mean and wicked, simply because they oppose them or their views on some subject. Those who oppose us are sometimes our best friends in disguise. When your Uncle was a callow youth, he fell clear up to his ears in love with a freckle-faced girl—but it was "sweetness wasted on the desert air," for she loved another, and the day they committed

matrimony in the first degree, your Uncle
thought them the meanest couple on earth.
He has often met that couple together with
their numerous progeny since that eventful
day, and he now feels like falling on the neck
of that man and weeping tears of joy down
his spine.   What was supposed to be an
injury was only made so by thinking.

My dear friends, you will see that your
thinking that the people you meet are mean
is about all the evidence you have that so
many are mean.   You should rejoice that
every person you meet does not agree with
you in your opinions, for some of your ideas
you will find to be very crude; and besides,
the world needs the diversity of opinions, of
acts, of plans, in order to bring about the
best results.

The lesson your Uncle wants to teach you
in this talk is to have faith in your fellow-
men.   Don't condemn the whole human race
because you meet a few people whom you
know to be absolutely mean.   Don't go
through this beautiful world wearing green
glasses and contending that everything you
see is green.   Don't go through the world
pulling the mote out of your neighbor's eye
while there is a beam in your own.   This

world has many good people. Are you
amongst the number?

STUDYING HUMAN NATURE.

My Dear Friends: Have you ever been a
student of human nature? Have you ever
noticed that the general make-up of people is
an index of what they will do or say? Of
course, education will do much toward
removing some inherent disposition to do
certain things, but not always.

Let us stroll down here on the corner and
observe the people that pass by.

Do you see that man coming there with
his toes turned in, or what is called pigeon-
toed?" Well, he is a man that cannot be
convinced. He knows it all, or at least knows
more than any other man can tell him. He,
in his mind, has had a wonderful experience,
and has done wonderful things in his time.

It is a waste of time to try to argue with or
convince men who walk that way. They
are one-idead.

Now, that man you see coming there with
his head above the level and chin pointing
forward is a person who wants to run things.
He wants to rule and if he can't do that he
tries to ruin; and that small, very small-eared
man passing by is so stingy that he won't
eat what his system demands. Such a man
will wear a dicky and grow a wart on the
back of his neck and use it for a collar button
to keep down expenses.

That woman who passed by just now was
about one step ahead of her husband. Did
you notice her lips? They are as thin as the
blade of a table knife. She has a ring in her
husband's nose, and those thin lips bespeak
a temper that is a terror to that poor man.
May the Lord have mercy on him when she
gets mad, for she will not.

Look at those two young women standing
there, each peeling a peach. Do you see that
one on the left cuts right in and throws half
the pulp away with the peeling? Well, she
has an extravagant nature and the young
man who commits matrimony with her wants
to have plenty about the larder. That other

one, you see, peels it so very thin. She has a very saving disposition.

Did you notice that man step clear to the edge of the sidewalk to let those ladies pass, while there was plenty of room for them to have turned to the other side a little and not crowded anyone? That man gets out of everybody's way. If those ladies had moved a little nearer to him he would have gotten clear off the walk. He is one of those men who feel like apologizing for being on earth. He never does anything of his own accord except get out of the way of others.

Look at that bald-headed man there who has just removed his hat. Do you observe how high his head is right at the middle point on top? A head like that denotes an extremist. When such men belong to church they can be heard half a mile when they pray and when they get mad at the church they can be heard swear at a greater distance. They generally talk loud and long. They are impulsive and apt to go to extremes when excited. They can't help it, for they were made that way.

Now, that fellow coming yonder striking his heels against the sidewalk instead of liftin them up is a poor shiftless man and will

always be so.   It is almost a waste of bread
for him to eat and live.   He does not amount
to anything.

There, do you not see that young lady
coming down the street, hippy-skippy-nippy-
nappy, swinging her head in every direction?
She is a silly little creature and would do well
enough if she would never grow old.   She
lacks stability.

There, did you hear those men laugh?
Did you observe that one of them hee-hawed
like a Balaam's ass?   Well, he is a coarse
man.   Now, that other man to his right who
broke forth at first with a loud laugh and
then tapered off to a simper, he always begins
a new job of work with a great spurt and
"peters out" before he gets through.   If he
decided to sow seventy-five acres of wheat
this fall, he went at it with a rush and the
first day or two he nearly killed his team.
But he concluded before he worked long that
fifty acres were enough, and when he quit he
found he had sown but twenty-five acres.

Have you noticed that fellow right there
by the corner who has stopped a half dozen
men as they came by, and drew them to one
side and talked in a tone so no one could hear
him except himself and the one to whom he

was talking? Now there are a few men who never talk to another without taking him to one side. Such men are not to be trusted. They are generally betrayers of confidence.

That man you see with one suspender, one pant leg in his boot and a general slovenly dress is a slouch. Just follow him to where his team is hitched and you will see that his harness are fitted on his horses in about the same style that his clothes are on him.

Look at that big fat man there in the center of that group. Why are so many gathered around him? Hear him laugh. He is one of those men who draw everybody around him on account of his happy disposition. No matter where he goes he will attract people. He is a sure cure for the "blues." He is better than medicine for soul-sick people. He is a benefactor to mankind and when he becomes helpless he ought to receive a pension.

My dear friends, if you will observe closely you can learn much concerning the character of those you meet. Your Uncle could point out many other indexes to character, but these will suffice. This variety of acts and dispositions is what gives unity to the human race. A rainbow of but one color would not be beautiful. If all men were alike, life would grow monotonous. No doubt, each one has a niche to fill—each one is a part of one stupendous whole.

"Out of earth's elements mingled with flame,
Out of life's compound of glory and shame,
Fashioned and shaped by no will of their own,
And helplessly into life's history thrown,
Born by the law that compels men to be,
Born to conditions they could not foresee—
John and Peter, Robert and Paul,
God in his wisdom created them all."

WHERE ARE THEY?

My Dear Friends: This evening as the clock on the shelf is ticking away the time and the cricket is chirping in the corner and the shades of night have gathered around, your Uncle has fallen into a dream of the past, and his thoughts go back to eastern Ohio to the scenes of his boyhood, and as he stands there in imagination, and looks around him, he asks himself the question, What has become of his early associates? Where are they who played with him when a boy? Where are they who were grown up men and women at that time? Where are the school teachers that ruled him in more ways than one? Where are they all gone and what are they doing this evening?

He wanders down to the little old Bethlehem church that stands amid the honey locusts near the bank of Sandy creek, and climbs over the fence and strolls through the graveyard, and he finds many of them there.

Yes, my dear friends, many of those with whom your Uncle was acquainted in his boyhood days lie there beneath the sod, "Careless alike of the sunshine and rain—each in his windowless palace of rest.''

He looks around him and on the marble slabs, he reads the date of birth and death, and in but few cases is there other memorial to testify that the inmates ever existed. But deep down in the very being of him who stands there, many of them live. Thoughts of bygone days come rushing back like the flow of the tide of ocean and many of those dead live again. Yonder monument marks the grave of father. Where is he? Does he not live in the very thoughts, deeds and actions to a certain extent of those he left behind? When the mind calls up in long review the forms of those it knew in youth, time itself has been annihilated and Then is Now.

But your Uncle must not hold you here too long. He now wends his way to the old Brown Frame school house. Here he taught his first term of school. Well does he remember the first morning of that eventful term. And as he stands upon that dividing line, the Present, and looks back through the kaleidoscope of time and views the scene as it then was, he returns again and asks himself, where are they who gathered there as

the pupils of the Brown Frame school? What
has become of those boys and girls who for
four years called your Uncle their teacher?
Where are they all? Were the lessons they
received such as to make them better as the
years went by? Where are they! Echo
answers. Your Uncle thinks of them as the
boys and girls of Brown Frame school and
not as grown up men and women as all are
who are yet alive.

And the Cross Road school where three
years were spent as teacher. Where are
those boys and girls that came with whoop
and hurrah on each morning? They are not
there now. In his imagination, he strolls by
and as the boys and girls at recess time who
now are there come up, he asks them if Coon
Bowers still attends school here. They tell
him that no such a boy belongs to Cross Road
school. He inquires after many others, but
they are not there now. They have gone
from there and that is all that he can learn—
but they have not gone from the memory of
him who asks the question, Where are they?

In his dream he is carried up to the site of
the old log school house. Here is where he
first made the discovery that there was such
a thing as a school in the world. He sees

the long slab, backless benches, the old box
sheet iron stove, the goose quill pen.   He
sees the form of Silas G—— the tyrant who
presided over the school and who "licked"
one of them on an average every five minutes
while he taught there.   There sit the Dicken
boys, the Gantzes, the Jeromes, the Dorises,
the Casselmans, the Eckleys, the Westfalls,
and eight or ten different breeds of Harshes.
Your Uncle can see them all and as he hears
the rod of that old master strike the ceiling
he shuts his eyes and curses in speechless
silence.   But that old master is not there
now.   The last that was heard of him, he
furnished the corpse for a funeral somewhere
in Iowa.   Nor are those boys there now.
Where are they gone?   Your Uncle occasionally meets one of them—but he is not a boy
any more.   His head is becoming silvered
and he is nearing the summit of life.   The
shadows of these boys will soon cease to point
westward.   Yes, these boys and girls have
gone from there and come back no more save
on memory's tide.

It is with melancholy pleasure that your
Uncle visits these scenes and inquires for the
"boys."   He has no regrets or no desire to
live over those days again except in memory.

He does not believe with those who think
that childhood is the happiest period of life.
He believes that life and its enjoyments should
increase as time goes by, else it is a dismal
failure.   If when we ask Where are they? a
feeling arises in us that our brightest days
are gone, then can we recite with the poet,

"Comfort? Comfort scorned of devils,
This is the truth that the poet sings,
That a sorrow's crown of sorrow
Is remembering happier things."

My dear friends, you each, no doubt, often
go back to the scenes of your childhood and
ask where are they whom you then knew.

STRAY THOUGHTS.

My Dear Friends: This evening while your Uncle is in his thinkshop looking over the timber at hand, he has concluded to pick up some of the scraps that are lying around and join them together for the inspection of his readers.

The first thought that he will present you is, that there is always two sides to every subject—the outside and the inside. An Irishman fresh from the old sod was employed to drive a stage coach across the country with a number of high-toned Americans in it. Pat drove along many miles until he at last came to a railroad crossing and seeing the sign "Look out for the locomotive," he stopped and yelling from the top of the coach to those within—"Will one of ye's plaze look out for the locomotive?" One of the party answered "Why don't you look yourself." Pat answered, "and how the divil am I to look out when I am not inside."

Just so in life, a subject appears very different to those who view it from the outside to what it does to those who view it from the inside.

To the man in the moon, the earth moves; while to those on earth, the moon moves.

So my dear friends, if you feel inclined to criticise the acts and motives of those who are acting for themselves in matters that are not interfering with your rights, bear in mind that you are doing so from a standpoint without, while they may be acting from within.

Less than four hundred years ago, Columbus was considered a fool and heretic for asserting that the earth is round, and to-day the teacher that would teach his pupils that it is any other shape would be expelled and possibly sent to the lunatic asylum for treatment.

When Robert Fulton built his boat the common herd called it "Fulton's Folly," and stood on the banks of the Hudson and hooted and jeered him. But it moved and now the white sails are spread on every sea.

When the first steamer was built to cross the Atlantic the crowd stood around and said "It can't be done." "No steamship can ever cross the ocean, and a learned (?) physician of England wrote a book showing the impossibility of such an adventure. Well, my dear friends, the first copy of that book was brought to America in that steamship.

When railroads were first talked of, it was declared that three miles an hour would be the fastest time they could ever make and that it would be forever impossible for a train to run on any but a straight track.

When Morse asked congress to appropriate $30,000 to assist him in building a telegraph line to experiment on his invention, one congressman suggested that they build a lunatic asylum for him and another sneeringly moved that they appropriate money to build a line to the moon.

But the trains are running at more than three miles an hour, go around curves, over hills and through mountains. The telegraph has been perfected, and time and space have been annihilated by it.

My dear friends, your Uncle has observed that on the dead snags and limbs of the tree of Knowledge are perched blind human owls who sit there and look wise and hoot at those who are trying to make improvements over what already exists. It has ever been thus. If you desire to pass through this world without being severely censured, follow the advice given by Pope in the couplet:

"Be not the first by whom the new is tried.
Nor yet the last to lay the old aside."

IF.

My Dear Friends: Did you ever observe what everlasting things hang on "IF?"

It stands between many a man and success. It is a thief that has stolen (in the minds of many) all earthly achievements and has left them—Jeremiah-like—doling out their lamentations. It is a tyrant, quite often, that banishes hope from the human heart and leaves it worse than dead. It is a vulture that preys upon the living, and too often a murderer of the holiest ambitions of the soul. It is the insurmountable wall that separates what is from what was hoped to be.

Yes, my dear friends, IF things were not as they are, what wonderful changes there would be.

IF your Uncle had not been born, he would not be at all; and IF he had been born a female he would have been your Aunt. IF the matter of gender was not as it is, what great changes there would be in the average human family.

IF Greece had never flourished, IF Rome had never been, IF Columbus had never been

born, IF Washington had never existed, IF
Lincoln had died in his infancy, who can
surmise what the result would have been?
IF slavery had never been introduced into
the American colonies—the late war would
never have been, and the average politician
in this country would be cut short of cam-
paign fuel for want of scarlet garments.

IF the surroundings were different the
results would be different, also.

Why, my dear friends, if we had been born
and reared in China, we would all be wearing
"pig-tails" and believing that our eternal happiness depends upon it. IF we had been
born and reared in India, we would all believe
in the transmigration of souls, and not a
mouthful of meat would ever find its way to
our stomachs. IF we had been born and
reared in Turkey, when the bells from the
towers of the mosques peal forth the hour of
high twelve, we would all stop, no matter
where we were, and return thanks to Allah.

"IF I had only improved my time while
young," says the aged man as he is nearing
the end of his journey, "my life would have
been more pleasant."

"IF I had only had enough money to have
purchased a block when the city was platted,"

sighs the street loafer, "I would now be wealthy."

"IF I had only married the judge," whisper the Maud Mullers, "I might be living differently."

"IF I had only followed my mother's advice," says the criminal, "I would not be where I am."

Thus it is all along the avenues of life we find men and women who are forever lamenting over the mistakes or supposed mistakes of their past lives. The hell-hounds of Regret and Remorse are forever dogging their steps or baying on their tracks. These people have turned their heads upon their shoulders and are gazing with sorrow into the land of WAS, and see nothing but the tombstones erected at the graves of disappointed hopes, which lie on either side of the pathway of life.

IF they would only look forward into the beautiful land of Will-be, and let "the dead past bury its dead," how much brighter and pleasanter would their lives be, and how much happier would they make those around them.

Since no one is permitted to choose his parents or to name the country where his eyes shall first behold the light of the sun, or to have choice as to the coloring matter that enters into his skin,—it is worse than folly for him to sit down and lament and groan, and say, "IF things had been different."

Your Uncle would not have you understand that he believes you should be contented with anything and everything that may come to you, for he verily believes that contentment as understood by most people is nothing more or less than satisfied laziness. But what he wants to impress upon you is, not to spend your time in grieving over the past mistakes of your life, and neglect the present and blast the hopes of your future.

When you have set your mark and feel certain it is a worthy one, then if you miss it, "Pick your flint and try it again."

When things do not go to suit you do not sit down and hold your jaw and whine about it until you become a being of disgust. But up and doing and profit by your mistake.

And now, my dear friends, your Uncle asks you to make use of that little word IF just as sparingly as possible, for those who use it to excess are generally hated and shunned by all good people.

"Look not mournfully into the past. It

comes not back again. Wisely improve the Present. It is thine. Go forth to meet the shadowy future without fear, and with a manly heart."

DRAG THE RAKE, BOYS.

My Dear Friends: When your Uncle was a mere boy working on the farm with his father and brothers many little incidents occurred which have since become lessons of profit.

One comes floating back this evening upon Memory's tide and serves as a text for your Uncle's Talk. In the year '63 or '64, wheat was worth $3 a bushel and farmers were anxious to save every head grown—but boys sometimes do not prove as frugal as their father would have them. Thus it was in this case. The wheat field was upon a hill-side. An older brother and a hired hand were cutting it with cradles, and a younger brother, his father and your Uncle were

raking the swathes into sheaves and binding
them. The hillside was so steep that the
grain could be cut but one way—hence the
cradlers when they cut through to the end
would walk back carrying their cradles.
Father would insist on the rakes being
dragged on our return to gather up the heads
of wheat that lay scattered about. He once
stopped at the end and when we trudged on
out of his sight, we shouldered our rakes and
let the scattered heads remain on the ground.

Presently a loud well-known voice rang
out from the knoll over which we had passed,
in tones which we did not mistake, "Drag
the rake, boys, wheat is $3 a bushel."

The voice of him who uttered that command has been stilled by the night of death,
but the wisdom which it contains is yet heard
through the trumpet of years.

My dear friends, there is quite a difference
between being heard and being understood.
If a person is not heard (unless his audience
be deaf) it is the fault of the speaker, if he is
not understood it is the fault of the hearer.

Well, your Uncle heard distinctly the
utterance, "drag the rake, boys," but it took
years to reach the seat of his understanding.
There is an excellent lesson in it—one which

when fully understood and practiced will be a benefit.

Look around you, my dear friends, and see how many persons there are who have shouldered their rakes instead of dragging them. See how many have gone through to the end of their swath and are now walking back with their rakes in the air. Not a head will they catch—not a kernel will they save. The world is full of people who do not drag their rakes,—and who will not even carry them on their shoulders, but have cast them aside and are sitting around claiming a right to a share of the sheaves bound and the grain gathered by those who drag their rakes.

There is another class of people who drag their rakes and will not lift them for stones or snags—but rip right through. Such people soon find all the teeth broken out of their rake and sometimes the head of it split, so new teeth cannot be inserted. Others drag their rake right through everything that comes in its way. The golden wheat, the rag-weed, the Canada thistle, the sand-burr and bull-nettle are all heaped together—one conglomerate mass—never to be separated.

The swath of life which every one has to cut and bind into sheaves can not always be untied. We can not walk back to the other end dragging our rakes, and come through again. The seed which we sow at seed time has much to do with the sheaves which we rake together and tie at harvest time. "Drag the rake, boys," through life. You may catch many a straw which may show you the direction of the wind or the course of the currents. Drag the intellectual rake, boys, and you will find occasionally an idea hanging to it.

The largest ear of wheat is not always found in the largest field nor will the largest rake always gather the greatest amount of grain.

There are some people who seem to think that there is no room for their rakes—that some other fellow has their swath—that the harvest is past and all the grain has been gathered, bound into sheaves, threshed and marketed, and they have arrived a little too late to get a share, so they stand around and in their disappointment and anger, they smash their rakes over the stumps and stones on the outside of the field, forgetting that they will need them when the season returns.

My dear friends, your Uncle admonishes you to drag the rake as you pass through life.   Drag the rake socially—drag the rake physically—drag the rake morally—drag the rake intellectually, and when you get through to the end of your swath you will have a crop of grain to thresh instead of chaff and cheat.

GROWING APART.

My Dear Friends: Away up in the Rocky Mountains you will find two little streams issuing from the rocks within a few miles of each other, and seeking to obey the law of gravitation, they wind around the little ravines eager to escape and become something greater.   These two streams form the head waters of the great rivers Columbia and Missouri.   As they proceed they grow farther apart until the waters of one is poured into the Pacific ocean—while the other courses its way east and south until swallowed up by the mighty Mississippi.

These inanimate beings obeyed the law of Nature and thus grew apart.

How like these mighty rivers are many human beings. Their sources may have been near each other—they may have been children of the same parents, reared and nurtured under the same roof—yet their courses in life may diverge as widely as the Columbia and Missouri.

Is it from some law of Nature which they are compelled to obey like the waters, or is it from some law of impulse? Or are they responsible for the course they pursue?

While people are like these rivers in one respect—they may differ in that they may grow apart in thought, feeling and action, and yet, in body, remain under the same roof and eat from the same table.

How often may be seen brothers who have been rocked in the same cradle—soothed and caressed by the same mother, growing apart until they lose all trace of each other save in memory. How often may be seen a young married couple starting out amid the mountains of hardship which so often rise before the poor in early life—but as the years roll on, and they have accumulated enough of this world's goods on which to live in ease, they have so grown apart in opinions and feeling that the streams of kindness and sympathy that flow from the heart never reach each other's heads. They have grown apart until the cold and sterile mountain that separates them is higher than the Rocky Mountains which separate the rivers referred to.

Into the stream of life many obstructions may be thrown to turn it from its course. Selfishness, cruelty and unkindness have caused many to grow apart who should have lived closely together. Greed for the accumulation of this world's goods has caused many a man to convert his head into an account book and his heart into a stone, and thus he has grown apart from the world into a piece of congealed self.

My Dear Friends, your Uncle would not have you believe that this growing apart is always a bad thing. It is as often a blessing as a curse. If you have bad associates whose influence has a tendency to drag you down, it is well to grow apart from them. Early associates are quite often a mill-stone around the neck of him who has an ambition to rise above the station in life occupied by mediocres.

But oftimes it is with a kind of sorrow that

one looks back through the kaleidoscope of years and follows the winding stream of life from then to now.

> "Where are the friends
> That to me were so dear,
> Long, long ago, long ago,"

comes like an echo to the soul of him who asks it, and he will find that there has been a wonderful growing apart as the years have gone by. Many of those friends in whom he confided, and almost lived, moved and had his being years ago, have grown so far away from him that they are now scarcely ever thought of.

The following beautiful poem which appeared in the Yankee Blade, from the pen of S. W. Foss, fully illustrates this growing apart. Read it carefully and bear in mind that WHAT you are is more important than WHERE you are.

ENOCH, CYRUS, JERRY AND BEN.

Enoch and Cyrus and Jerry and Ben
Were babies together, four fat little men,
Four bald-headed babies, who bumped themselves
    blue,
And sprawled, grabbed and tumbled as all babies
    do—
Full of laughter and tears, full of sorrow and glee,
And big, bouncing bunglers as all babies be.
All in the same valley lived these little men—
Enoch and Cyrus and Jerry and Ben.

Enoch and Cyrus and Jerry and Ben
Were fast little chums—till they grew to be men.
Eight bare little feet on the same errands flew
Thro' meadows besprinkled with daisies and dew;
They were aimless as butterflies, thoughtless and
    free
As the summer-mad bobolink, drunken with glee.
A wonderful time were those careless days then
For Enoch and Cyrus and Jerry and Ben.

Enoch and Cyrus and Jerry and Ben
Grew from babies to boys, and from boys into men.
Too restless to stay in the circumscribed bound
Of the green hills that circled their valley around,
To the North and the South and the East and the
    West,
Each departed alone on a separate quest,
Ah! they'll never be the same to each other again—
Enoch and Cyrus and Jerry and Ben.

Enoch and Cyrus and Jerry and Ben,
Though companions in youth, were strangers as
    men;
Enoch grew rich and haughty and proud,
While Cyrus worked on with the toil driven crowd;
In the councils of state Jerry held a proud place,
But poor Ben, he sounded the depths of disgrace.
Ah! diverse were the lives of these boys from the
    glen—
Enoch and Cyrus and Jerry and Ben.

Enoch and Cyrus and Jerry and Ben,
Who can read the strong fates that encompassed
    these men?
The fate that raised one to the summit of fame,
The fate that dragged one to the darkness of shame!
Ah! silence is best; neither glory nor blame
Will I grant to the honored or dishonored name.
We are all like these boys who grew into men—
Enoch and Cyrus and Jerry and Ben.

PUBLIC SPEAKING AND PUBLIC SPEAKERS.

My Dear Friends: When your Uncle was a boy on the farm, he used to go to the fields and drive the cows home at milking time. He often observed that while the cows kept in the path that led to the barnyard, they would often reach first to this side and then to that and bite off a mouthful of grass and eat it as they passed along. Now and then they would break away from the path and run back, and the driver would have to go after them and bring them up again.

In many ways some public speakers are like these cows. They start out on the path of their subject which ought to lead them to the barnyard of conclusion where the cream and milk of their efforts can be extracted and used as intellectual food for their hearers. But they keep biting off a mouthful here to one side of their subject, and one there on the other side, and then break and run back to where they began, and their audience must follow them back and come over the same path again, and quite often they never reach the barnyard at all.

In fact, they fume and fuss and fight the air in wild gesticulation and bellow like cattle in those seasons of the year when they are bothered with warbles and gad-flies.

If it were not for the constitutional right to free speech and the liberty of the hearers to leave the place where some speakers speak, your Uncle would be in favor of having some speakers arrested for cruelty to animals.

First, your Uncle verily believes that there is too much public speaking in the present age for the welfare of good thinking. The average person is too apt to let the public speaker do his thinking for him. Figuratively speaking, the intellectual (?) morsel is chewed and the hearer closes his eyes and opens his mouth and swallows it down, not even tasting it,—thus bringing upon himself mental dyspepsia.

But as speakers are like the poor—always with us—it may be well for your Uhcle to point out some of the different kinds that are met, and in doing so he will use a classification made by John Hall in which he divides them into three great classes:

First, those who have NOTHING to say, and say it.

Second, those who have something to say, but do not say it.

Third, those who have SOMETHING to say, and say it.

The first class may be among the weak things of this earth which have been chosen to confound the mighty—but it is' doubtful. How often are we compelled, out of what is called courtesy, to sit and listen to mere sounds from a speaker whose talk is full of "airy nothings." He may be carrying a double head of steam, as it were, but his intellectual steam chest is so small and his escape valve so large that everything escapes in noise, and no power is left to move his audience. This class of public speakers who have nothing to say, and who say it, is quite numerous, and makes considerable noise while doing it too.

The second class—those who have something to say but do not say it—makes your Uncle very uneasy when he listens to one of them, and he always wishes that he could help him out in some way. This class is very small, for when a person really has something to say he can generally express it and in such a manner as to be understood, too.

The third class is always appreciated, whether what they say coincides with one's

views or not—whether what he says makes
one angry or not. At least, one thing is
certain, his audience will know what he said
and how he said it. This class always has a
clear conception of what they are saying and
feel, at least for the time, just what they are
talking about.

There are many things to which your Uncle might call your attention. There is the
public speaker who hems and haws and
apologizes and squirms around for ten or fif-
teen minutes when he first gets up, until his
audience begins to feel that he will never get
started. No public speaker has a moral right
to do this, even if he has the privilege. If
he is billed to speak, he should proceed at
once, or else say he is unprepared and sit
down. Silence is sometimes the finest ora-
tory your Uncle has ever heard.

Then there are those who never know when
to stop when they get started. They want to
exhaust the whole subject and their audience
too, and generally do the latter. At intervals
in the last half hour they say, "one thought
more" and "finally" and "in conclusion"
and "take the subject home with you," etc.
until the audience twist and squirm, yawn
and breathe "how long, O Lord! how long

will it be till this speaker stops;'' and when they get out of the hall, they take a solemn vow that they will never be bored again by that man.

Then there is the public speaker who seems to think that the louder he talks the greater impression he will make upon his audience. He will howl and saw the air, and then want people to be persuaded by what he says. Do you know that such a speaker is scarcely ever heard? In less than five minutes the majority of his audience hear nothing save the roar of the wind and seem to have gone into a kind of reverie.

My dear friends, there are volumes that might be said on this subject, but suffice it by saying that every public speaker should know what he wants to say and say it—he should study his subject in a two-fold relation so what he says may be applicable to his subject and audience,—he should not go into detail but suggest thought that will lead his hearers to think more than he has said—he should never attempt to relate a funny story unless he is certain that he can do it—he should look at his audience while talking— he should leave his audience when it is eager to hear him talk longer.

My dear friends, if any of you desire to become a public speaker study a few of the above suggestions and observe the weaknesses of other speakers and profit by them and then sail in.

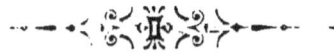

SEEING.

My Dear Friends: When your Uncle was a country schoolboy, he had the good fortune of attending several terms to a teacher who was able to think beyond the text-book—a thing which is rather uncommon among average teachers.

One day this teacher informed his school that people do not see with their eyes—but all sight (understanding) is in the mind, and by illustration and demonstration, he proved the truth of his assertion. He proved to us that there were many things before us that were unintelligible to us, and which could only be seen by the mind or understanding brought into the proper relation by the cultivation of the intellect.

My dear friends, the eye is only the camera obscura on which the picture is thrown—the mind sees the picture. Not all that falls upon the camera is seen.

The story of the six blind men who went to see the elephant, and who touching different parts of him formed different notions of that animal, is as applicable to people with eyes as it is to those blind men.

A few years ago the battlefield of Waterloo was visited by excursionists. Amongst them was an ignorant sight-seer who had more money than brains. The field was covered with briars and shrubs. The more intelligent of the party looked back through the telescope of history and saw the armies of the Duke of Wellington and the mighty Napoleon arrayed in bloody conflict—they saw the defeat of the French general and his army—they saw him as he was borne away in lonely exile to the island of St. Helena, there to eke out his life —they saw mighty governments change as the result of this battle, and while they looked and conversed, the ignorant boor who was with them, exclaimed: "I do not see anything wonderful in a few briars and shrubs to go into fits about."

His eyes beheld—but his mind did not see.

There was an excursion of the learned to Niagara Falls a few years ago, and as it passed through Buffalo, New York, a Vermonter —a sheep man who had brought a carload of sheep to the Buffalo market—joined the excursion. He was one of those men who is in love with his business. No matter what he looked at, he saw something that reminded him of SHEEP. When the excursion reached the Falls, and each was viewing the sublimity and grandeur of this mighty freak of Nature, —the force of gravity was seen as never before—in the spray the beautiful rainbow revealed all the primitive colors, and the scientists saw the laws of physics obeyed to the letter and while they were standing there awe-stricken with the sight, the old Vermonter with his pantaloons in his boots— with his hands up to his elbows in his pockets—blurted out, "My God! What a good place this would be to wash sheep."

He had eyes, but he saw not above or beyond. He could see nothing of what the others saw, for his mind was uncultivated and concentrated in the horned patriarch of the sheep tribe.

My dear friends, education is the telescope that reveals thousands upon thousands of things to mankind. With it a person may read sermons in the pebbles and find companions in the babbling waters of the brook. By education, man may see to read the starry sky—by education he can go down into the bowels of the earth and see the past history of the rocks—by education he can see the morsel of food transformed to living tissue—by education he can bring up in long review the nations of the earth that have flourished and faded—by education the mental horizon may be so enlarged, that seeing may not be confined simply to the present, but may be extended through the mists of bygone years.

My dear friends, if you desire to "have eyes and see not," just cease to cultivate your mind. If you wish to go through this life like a young robin—with your eyes closed and mouth open—do not improve your intellect, but if you wish to see the beauties that lie around you on every side, improve your mind, and the panorama will present itself at every turn.

WHAT MAN CAN DO.

My Dear Friends: If you will cast your eye over the progress of the past century you will almost be led to the conclusion that man is capable of doing anything that he desires. He has caged steam and by its expansive force, he sends the iron horse prancing across the continent. He has tamed lightning and by the telegraph he has annihilated time and space. He has by the invention of the telephone made it possible to' converse in audible tones for hundreds of miles. He has spanned the mighty rivers with bridges, tunneled the mountains, and no obstacle seems to arise that he cannot surmount.

But, my dear friends,—your Uncle has observed that with all man's boasted ability —with all the progress he has made in science, art, literature or in any direction whatever—after all he can do but two things. Namely: Put things together and take things apart.

The farmer can do no more than put the seed into the ground—or put the seed and the ground together—he cannot make it grow. Nature does that. Man builds railroads, and all he does is to place the ties and earth together to form the roadbed, he joins the irons together to make the track. If he wants to span the rivers with bridges, he only puts things together—he creates nothing. He tunnels mountains by taking rocks and earth apart. He enslaves the winds to do his work by bringing his wheel in contact with the atmosphere. He produces all these changes by either mechanical or chemical force. He kindles the fire—but the chemical change called combustion produces the heat. He puts cold water and cold lime together, and Nature slacks it. He, in fact, is but an agent to guide and direct force—he can not create it.

Things must be put together, else no effect will be produced, and if put together in their proper relations the effect will produce what is called good—if put together improperly the effect will produce what is called evil.

The same knife that cuts your bread may cut your throat. It is the application—the putting together—that produces the effect, and not the things themselves.

My dear friends, let us observe if the same statement, that man can do but two things, will hold good in literature.

You are aware that the letters of the alphabet have no power—no meaning in fact when detached. But just put them together in proper relation and they form every word in the English language, whether that word be good or bad. A good word may be so put together with other words as to make its meaning bad.

Every sentence uttered or written can only be done so by putting words together. The same word when joined differently may produce a different thought.

The following sentences convey quite different meanings although made up of the same words: "Lost, a cow with brass knobs on her horns, belonging to a widow." "Lost, a cow belonging to a widow with brass knobs on her horns." The meaning depends on the manner in which the words are put together and not on the words themselves.

The sentence, "Woman—without her—man would be a savage," does not mean the same as the sentence, "Woman without her man—would be a savage."

You see, my dear friends, that there is much in the statement that man can do but two things, and if he does those well he will, no doubt, fill his mission on earth. Everything in Nature is governed by immutable laws, and Man progresses just in proportion as he discovers these laws and applies the proper principles to make them serve his wants.

If your Uncle has caused you to think by the few thoughts presented above, he has accomplished his desire.

CONVERSATION.

My Dear Friends: Conversation is quite often confounded with talking,—but there is a vast distinction between the two terms. The former implies at least two persons who speak and listen alternately, while the latter implies a speaker and a listener. There is no way in which so much information can be gained—no way in which so much happiness can be derived—no way in which so much misery can be inflicted as there can be by conversation.

It is often the block and tackle that raises people to higher planes of thought or the millstone about the neck that drags them down to gross and groveling things.

The subjects of conversation may be divided into two classes, namely: persons and things; and these may be subdivided into an innumerable number according to their treatment.

Your Uncle has observed that the common herd of mankind prefers to converse about PERSONS instead of things, and that, too, when the subject of their conversation is not present. Just listen to the ordinary conversation, and after the greeting and reference to the weather are made, then you will hear the name or names of parties not present referred to, and that quite often in uncomplimentary terms. People fall into the habit of directing their conversation about other people who, in their opinion, have shortcomings, and great delight seems to be taken in showing them up in the worst possible light. Women, as a class, are given to this kind of conversation more than men.

Now, my dear friends, the last sentence above will cause your Uncle to be discussed, if not cussed, instead of conversing on the thought presented in that sentence.

How often do people meet and converse for
hours and hours about some one whom they
consider worthless, insignificant and mean,
and with whom they would not associate,
and yet they will waste valuable time which
in no way will benefit themselves or the
person of whom they are conversing.   There
is scarcely a private social gathering where
the character of some absent one or ones is
not picked, carved and dissected in a most
unmerciful manner,—beheading people, as it
were, with the tongue.

Your Uncle one time offered to give a
present to each of a party of young folks who
the next day intended to have a social gathering, provided they would let their conversation be wholly about things instead of
absent persons.   The presents have not yet
been called for.

Why is it that so many good people will
spend their time and destroy their peace of
mind in conversing about other people of
whom they know so little?   Why condemn
people when the circumstances and surroundings which make them what they are, are
illy understood?   Why assassinate an absent
person with your tongue and then when you
meet him, greet him with a smile and shake

his hand and inquire about his health? What
good can come of speaking disparagingly of
other people when you hope and trust what
you have said will never be heard by them?
Should your criticism not be, first for the
benefit of him who is criticised, and second
for the benefit of society?

How different is conversation which dis-
cusses things instead of persons. Of course
it takes more thought—more knowledge—
more education—more moral character—
more brains generally to converse on subjects
of this kind—the benefits and pleasures
derived are far greater in the end.

The reason there are so many poor conver-
sationalists is because people have devoted
most of their time to business matters, and
but little time to the study of science, art and
literature. Men have fallen into the habit,
not into the idea, that it is necessary to
devote every moment to their business matters, and hence their conversations when
away from their place of business takes
naturally in that course. The school teacher
talks school, the lawyer talks law, the physician talks disease, the minister talks sin and
righteousness, the farmer talks crops and
hogs, the dry goods man talks calico and

silk, and so on through all the callings in life until every person's conversation smells of his profession or trade. Would it not be better to direct the mind when away from business by conversation which will open up new channels of thought? To be a good conversationalist—a rare thing—one must possess a broad and liberal education. One must know that "all right thinking people" do not necessarily think as he does, and that in the continent of Thought there is room for every explorer.

RESOLUTIONS.

My Dear Friends: You, no doubt, have observed that there never has been a time in the history of the world when so many resolutions have been passed as in the present age. Resolutions full of nothing—resolutions which are to be put in print instead of into practice—resolutions which are intended to boom their author instead of benefitting the convention which passes them—resolutions which will not bear the light of reason to fall upon them—resolutions which are never thought of before or after the day they are adopted.

This passing of resolutions which are not put into action has a demoralizing influence upon those who adopt them, yet your Uncle believes that while the practice of passing resolutions without due consideration is continued it is best that they are not carried out.

A resolution—and when your Uncle says resolution here he means resolution—presupposes that thought has preceded and that action will follow, else the resolution is only another name for falsehood.

"Think, resolve, act," is a good motto

when taken in its order, but when reversed
it ofttimes proves disastrous. How often do
you see men who ACT the fool and then RE-
SOLVE that they will never do so again, but
never put their resolution into effect. It is
much easier to attend a temperance convention and arise and offer a resolution condemn-
ing the liquor traffic and then go home and
sit down and see the law violated daily, than
to do anything to put the resolution into
action.

The world is full of moral cowards who
want to be dead certain that a large majority
will favor the enforcing of a resolution before
they will commit themselves.

Resolutions passed in a convention too
often contain narrow opinions which are
either the fruits of some contracted mind or
the legitimate works of the devil.

A number of years ago, a national convention of a small sect was called to meet at
Memphis, Tennessee; and when the time
came there were but three ministers present.
One of them was elected chairman, and he
appointed the other two a committee on resolutions. The committee withdrew from the
hall and in a short time returned and reported
the following:

"Your committee beg leave to make the following report:

1. Resolved that the world belongs to the Saints.

2. Resolved that we three are the Saints."

The report was unanimously adopted and the convention adjourned.

My dear friends, these resolutions like many others prove nothing—in fact, in the true sense of the term, are not resolutions at all.

Nine-tenths of the resolutions passed are the ebullition of anger, the effervescence of impulsive natures, the froth of ignorance or the snares of the hypocrite.

Resolutions are not confined to the living alone—but to the dead also. Just how a series of resolutions can do the dead any good is more than your Uncle has been able to comprehend. If people or societies have such an exalted opinion of a person why should they wait until he dies before they formulate them into resolutions, prefaced by a number of "whereases." No criticism is intended upon a tribute of respect given to the world by the friends of the dead—but many of the resolutions passed on such occasions are but the vapor of a momentary impulse.

My dear friends, do not infer that your Uncle is advising you not to make any resolutions. Far from that, he would have you first think, then resolve, then act, and when you find that you have make a bad resolution do not be foolish enough to act in accordance.

It is the actions—not the resolutions—of men that emblazon their names on the pages of the world's history.

Bear in mind that there is quite a difference between RESOLVING to do right and DOING it.

FORMERS AND REFORMERS.

My Dear Friends: Your Uncle has always believed that there is a great deal of time spent in trying to RE-form parties and people that could be better employed in forming them correctly in the first place. Men go howling around the country about the need of reform who make no effort to see that the children of their own household are forming habits that will not need RE-forming in after life.

The building of a man or woman is not the work of a day—but of a lifetime, and the idea held out by many that a reformed man is just as good as one who has always walked somewhere near the path of right and duty, is a false light that is leading too many into the swamp of evil habits from which they never return.

Figs do not grow on cactus nor are Ben Davis apples found on the crab tree.

The seed sown prophesies the harvest and the wild-oats sown in youth will not produce a valuable crop of manhood or womanhood.

The growing of a manhood or womanhood must be done on the same principle as improving a Kansas farm, and that is hard work and patient toil in its cultivation.

The sand-burrs of an evil inclination must be rooted out—the bull nettles of an ungovernable temper must be brought under control—the Canada thistles of avarice and discontent must be grubbed out and the weeds of various kinds that are to be found in human nature must be plowed up, so the sunshine may beam down upon better things and the gentle rains may do their work in bringing forth an abundant harvest of good deeds and acts.

It is much easier to be a re-former than a former, because it is much easier to find fault with a job after it is completed than it is to do the work.

It is much easier to inform people wherein they erred than it is to point out the way and direct children how to avoid error. It is easier to get people to listen to the sins and short-comings of others than it is to instruct them how to avoid the same. It is much easier to point the finger of scorn at the wart on the other fellow's nose than it is to remove the wart or prevent its growing in the first place.

My dear friends, your Uncle would not have you infer that he does not believe in a person reforming who has done wrong and led a bad life,—but he has little if any use for a REFORMED REFORMER. Society seems to be eager to lionize a man especially who has touched the shoals and depths of wickedness and who reforms and uses it as capital to bring him into prominence.

Does a person deserve any special credit for doing his duty to society by conducting himself properly?

Has a reformed reformer any moral right to inflict upon an audience a recital of his past life, with all its horrors, and then with a kind of pharisaical air pat himself on the back and say, "I thank Thee that I am not as other men are."

My dear friends, there is an old saying that the way to reform a man is to reform his grandparents, and your Uncle has a great deal of faith in the idea. The lives of men and women reach back through many generations. Unseen hands quite often push us on to do the deeds and acts performed.

Your Uncle once listened to the great (?) Francis Murphy recite the horrors of his past life—a life steeped in murder and debauchery. He told of the many nights he had gone home drunk, and driven his wife and children from the house, fleeing for their lives, and then drawing himself in an attitude of "now-look-how-big-a-man-I-am," he seemed to act as though he thought it necessary to be mean first in order to be good.

As your Uncle listened to him, he thought to himself, "I do not want any such a man to teach me how to treat my wife."

The man who plants an orchard, cultivates and prunes the trees, and guards the jack-rabbits from peeling them will have a far better orchard, other things equal, than he

who plants the trees and takes no care of
them.   Just so it is in the forming of a manhood or womanhood, it needs constant care
by those in charge—whether that be the
parents or self.

There is need of reformers, but it is doubtful if the world needs REFORMED reformers
who saw the air in recitation of their past
iniquity.   Rotten timber must sometimes be
removed from the building—but it should not
be used by others in the construction of their
homes.

Bad habits must also be abandoned and
mistakes corrected—but they should so far as
possible not be ingrafted on others or used as
stock for self-aggrandizement.   Let there be
more time and care given to the formation of
character and less time will be needed for
re-formation.

HOME OVER HERE.

My Dear Friends: When your Uncle Jonas was a tender youth, he used to attend meeting at a little country church which the common herd called the "Devil's Half Acre," —but its proper name was Emery Chapel. Often has he heard men and women speak of what they expected that home to be and how they longed to go and enjoy it. He has seen and heard men sing and talk about their "Home Over There" who never made an effort to build for themselves and family a decent and comfortable "Home Over Here." They seemed to forget that the only way to build for the future home is to work and do what is right in the present one.

Our home over here should be made one of the most pleasant places on this side of the pearly gates of the New Jerusalem, and it can be made so if all the members of the home work to make it so.

Too many children in this age are growing up almost ignorant of what home is. They have been hauled about in a covered wagon from place to place until they become uneasy and do not want to settle down for a permanent home.

The home over here that is purchased is not half so good as one that is built by father and mother and the children. It is a happy feeling to the man who can sit under a tree in his own door yard and say "I planted this tree." It is a great pleasure for the members of the home to know and feel that the orchard, grove, vineyard and berry patch were all planted, nurtured and cared for by them. You never saw a renter take much interest in the property he has in charge. You never saw a man "shoulder a musket to defend a boarding house," but a home he will die for if he is a man of honor.

When your Uncle refers to the home over here he does not mean the building, or what is too often called a residence. A home often means something quite different from that. Upholstered furniture, lace curtains, lambrequins, tidies and Brussels carpet, are too often found in houses which are considered too fine for a home, and children are almost compelled to remove their shoes before entering, so they may not soil the fixtures. Children soon become dissatisfied with such surroundings and seek to spend their spare moments elsewhere.

A great many men are so engrossed with their business that they have no time to spend in making a happy home, and becoming acquainted with their children. A story is told of a man of this kind, who thought more of making money than of building a home. During the week he rose early before his little son was out of bed, his wife would get his breakfast and he would go to his place of business—take his dinner at a restaurant and return late, after his little boy had gone to bed. Sunday was the only day he could spend with his family. He slapped his little son one day and the child went into the house crying, and when asked by his mother what the matter was, he said, "That man who boards here on Sunday slapped me."

If our home over here is to be what it should be—what it may be—there must be no room in the house too good to use—the members of the household must feel and know that they each own a part of the home. Children must be taught to obey—for boys and girls who are permitted to do as they please before they have grown to years of discretion do not honor their father and mother for it. Kind words and kind acts should not be forgotten in the home over here. The man who ruthlessly wounds the members of his household with cross or unkind words—the woman who finds fault with everything and everybody around her family circle, ought to get a free pass to their home over there where fuel is reported to be cheaper than it is here in Kansas.

Your Uncle has observed men who have sacrificed their homes—who have destroyed the peace and happiness of those they loved, all for strong drink. These men vowed when at the marriage altar that they would "love, cherish and protect," and yet they seem to be unable to control themselves and to make their home over here a fit dwelling place for their families.

My dear friends, the building of a home requires constant care. It requires patience and forbearance. It requires the highest order of government—which is granting to others the privileges you ask for yourself under like circumstances. To furnish food, clothing and shelter for wife and children and that alone, are not all the requirements of a home. You do the same for your hogs, cattle and horses. But the sunlight of love must shine around the home circle—brute fear must be banished—kindness must be there—amusements must be tolerated and the little courtesies of life must not be neglected if our home over here is to be a fit dwelling place. Let greater care be taken to beautify this home.